Ca

2637

Carlson, Dale Bick
Perkins the Brain

Date Due

Curtis			
3			
Curtis			

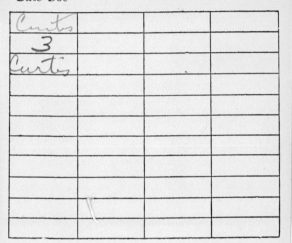

A nine-year-old tries to prove his worth to a new gang.

Library Form 10

Date Due

PERKINS THE BRAIN

PERKINS
THE BRAIN

by Dale Bick Carlson

illustrated by Albert W. D. Carlson

DOUBLEDAY & COMPANY, INC.

GARDEN CITY, NEW YORK

LIBRARY OF CONGRESS CATALOG CARD NUMBER 64–11704
COPYRIGHT © 1964 BY DALE BICK CARLSON

FOR OUR SON
DANIEL BICK CARLSON

CONTENTS

PERKINS THE BRAIN

1. THE NEW PLACE

When Perkins moved to a new house in a new town, he decided the best thing to do was to look around the place first. Perkins figured you have to see which houses on the street have kids, and how many, and how old. Then you have to see which gang you want to join.

Perkins was nine. He thought it was a good age to be moving into a new place, because you have choices. When you were nine, you could either be the oldest of the smaller kids or the youngest of the bigger kids.

Mrs. Jones, Perkins's mother, was fluttering over tissue paper and packing crates.

"Don't you think you better leave all that stuff until we see whether the people around here are okay?" suggested Perkins.

"But this is a *nice* neighborhood," replied his mother. She was trying to remember where she had packed the living-room lamp shades. "I'm sure everybody will be lovely."

"Lovely!" said Perkins in disgust. "I hope not."

"Go along now," scolded Allie, who had been

the Jones's cook forever and ever. "Don't bother your mother this afternoon. She's got enough to do 'thout you talking nonsense."

Sometimes Perkins worried about his parents. They were swell parents, but Perkins wasn't always absolutely certain that they were exactly bright. When his father had told Perkins and Mrs. Jones that they were going to move, Perkins asked why—naturally. His father, who was a General Practitioner (which is a long way of saying he was a Doctor), said that the new place would be a better town to be a doctor in.

"Why?" Perkins had asked. "Is everybody sicker there?"

Frankly, the thought of moving in with a lot of people who had measles and things all the time didn't appeal to him too much.

But his father had said no, that wasn't the reason. It was just that there weren't enough doctors in the new town, and he thought he could be useful.

"But if nobody's sick, they don't need a doctor," argued Perkins.

His father only laughed and rumpled Perkins's hair. And when his father rumpled Perkins's hair, Perkins knew that the discussion had ended—but definitely.

Then the movers had come, and everything that belonged to Dr. and Mrs. Willoughby Jones, including their son Perkins, had been moved to the new house.

Perkins thought he would just climb up to the attic and take a look. You never could tell what the first people might have left behind. There was an old trunk with some magazines and a few pieces of string in it. The magazines might have some pretty interesting pictures in them, and string always came in handy. Perkins carried the stuff down to his room to sort through later on. He saved almost everything like that, since you never knew when something was likely to be useful or even valuable. Then he went back up to the attic. The only other good thing up there was a chair with one leg missing. But if you balanced carefully, you could sit on it fine. Perkins dragged it over to the window so he could start checking over the neighborhood.

The shape of the street looked all right for riding his bicycle on, not too smooth, with enough bumps at least to put some excitement into the thing. There were eight houses, so Perkins figured the percentage on kids ought to be good even though he couldn't see any. They must be sitting around somebody's back yard. All of the houses but two had flower gardens. That meant only two dogs. People who had flower gardens didn't usually have dogs and vice versa. So far the score was two–one in favor of the place, which wasn't too bad. But of course he hadn't met any of the kids yet, and that counted most when you added things up—maybe five, maybe ten points right there.

Perkins sat at the window for a while longer, counting up points. Half a point here for a garden hose that ought to be a pretty good squirter when it got hot out, two points there for a pogo stick in somebody's front yard he might be able to borrow, one point more for a window ledge where some fresh cookies were cooling. He only gave that one point, since you never knew whether they were the kind of people who gave you some to taste. Then he had to subtract a point when he caught sight of one of the dogs. It was a poodle with one of those silly hair cuts. A dog like that wasn't any use to anybody.

Ding-a-ling! Ding-a-ling! An ice-cream wagon came round the corner. In two seconds it had disappeared from sight behind a bunch of kids. For a while, Perkins couldn't sort them out too well since they were all together. Then he couldn't tell much about them, since all they did was sit around and eat their ice cream. Perkins wouldn't have minded some ice cream himself. But he didn't feel the time had come yet for him to go out. Buying an ice cream wasn't much of a way to introduce yourself. Everybody did that.

So he watched some more. There were four older kids who looked like they might be eleven,

and who might just possibly let him play with them. If he wanted to. There were four kids about his own age, maybe a little more, maybe a little less. There were three really small kids, who probably just got in the way, and one baby, which counted for nothing at all.

"Sure is mean of them to go on eating all that ice cream when I haven't got any," said Perkins to himself.

Then he remembered that they didn't even know he was alive. That made Perkins feel kind of small and lonely. A lump came to his throat when he thought about how he didn't know any of the kids in this new place.

But they don't know *me* either, considered Perkins. And that sort of evened it up a little.

After awhile the kids started doing things instead of just sitting there and eating ice cream. That was better. Perkins could see more what they were like.

Somebody's mother called, "HenRY! Henry, come here."

Henry ran so fast—in the opposite direction—that Perkins knew he wasn't going to be the fastest runner on the block. There were maybe five kids who were taller, so he wasn't the tallest. He obviously wasn't the smallest, either. He wasn't the oldest, nor the youngest. He wasn't the fattest, nor the skinniest, or even the most in-between. He didn't have the only bicycle and he didn't even own a pogo stick. It was sickening. He was going to have to be *something* the most if he was going to make any impression at all.

Perkins watched out the window some more. It wasn't really too interesting because nobody was doing anything special, just sitting around. The four kids his age were yelling a little, but not very loud. It was then that Perkins decided what he would be. If he couldn't be the fastest or the tallest or anything like that, he would be the brainiest.

"And since you never know what's going on in the minds of older people who are eleven or so," decided Perkins, "if I'm going to be the brainiest, I better stick with the kids my own age."

Perkins's last idea on the subject was, "They look all right. At least they're yelling a lot."

2. GETTING BRAINS

It was much easier to decide you were going to be brainy than to figure out how you got that way. Perkins thought he'd ask around.

His mother was in the living room, making out her marketing list. Perkins watched for a while. Anybody who could spell that fast must know something about brains.

"Where did you get your brains?" Perkins asked.

"Don't be rude, Perkins dear," said his mother absently. "What a good idea for dinner," murmured Mrs. Jones to herself and wrote down Brains—In Wine Sauce on her list.

"I'm not being rude. I want to know," explained Perkins. It was hard talking to mothers sometimes. They always thought you were either being rude or getting sick.

But it was important, so he tried again. "How do you get brains?"

"Why you're either born with brains or you're not," said Mrs. Jones.

"Was I born with brains?" asked Perkins hopefully. If he was already born with brains, he wouldn't have to go to the trouble of getting any.

His mother patted his cheek. "You are a nice, sweet boy, and Mother doesn't care whether you have brains or not."

Perkins decided what his mother meant was, he wasn't born with too many brains. And the other part, about being a nice, sweet boy, was all right for his mother to think. But it wasn't the sort of thing Perkins wanted to be known for *generally* speaking.

Maybe he had better call his father on the telephone.

"That you, Daddy?" said Perkins.

"Yes, it's me," answered Dr. Jones cheerfully. "What can I do for you, son?"

"How do you get brains?" asked Perkins.

"Well," said his father. "That's quite an important question."

Perkins was so pleased he tied a few knots in the telephone cord.

"I'd say," continued Dr. Jones, "that there are two ways to get brains."

Perkins felt so good he put a pencil in each one of the knots he had tied in the telephone cord. It looked pretty snazzy that way.

"What's the first way?" asked Perkins.

"The first way," said his father, "is to read a lot and learn other people's ideas."

Perkins wasn't too fond of reading. So he asked what was the second way to get brains.

"The second way is to sit down and think up a lot of new, original ideas yourself. That's even harder."

"Okay," said Perkins. "Thanks."

"You're welcome," said his father and hung up the telephone.

Perkins went up to his room and sat down to think. He untied his shoelaces a couple of times, and tied them again in different ways. But he couldn't think of a new way to tie them, and besides, what was so original about tying your shoelaces anyway.

It was hard work, thinking up new, original ideas. It was even harder work sitting still long enough to think. All that work was making Perkins hungry, so he thought he'd go down to the kitchen for a peanut butter sandwich.

"It may not be new and original," said Perkins. "But it's still a good idea."

Allie was putting away all the things that had come from the market. When she heard the kitchen door slam, she said immediately, "Peanut butter to the RIGHT," without even turning around.

"How'd you know it was me?" said Perkins.

"It's right before your lunch, ain't it?" grumbled Allie. "Who else comes in the kitchen this time of

day and ruins his lunch. Don't take no brains to figure that out."

"You have brains, Allie?" asked Perkins casually.

"Sure 'nough do," said Allie.

Perkins poked a hole through his peanut butter sandwich and licked his finger.

"You going to ruin your appetite," clucked Allie.

Perkins ignored this. Everyone in the whole house knew Perkins could eat an *elephant* and not ruin his appetite.

"How do you get brains, Allie?" asked Perkins.

"I buys 'em," said Allie. "Them's brains right there, that package on the sink."

Perkins got even more casual. "What are you going to do with them, those old brains?"

"Cook 'em," replied Allie. "For dinner."

Perkins was flabbergasted. Here was he, Perkins, walking around needing brains. And people who had all the brains they could use were just going to eat these brains like any old lamb chop.

And why hadn't anybody told him about being able to buy brains? All that stuff about having to be born with them and having to think a lot, when all you really had to do was order them from the market with the lettuce and ketchup.

At lunch, for the first time since he was born, Perkins didn't have very much appetite. His mother noticed it immediately.

"He must be sick," said Mrs. Jones, feeling

Perkin's forehead to see if he had any temperature.

"He certainly looks a little green to me," said Dr. Jones.

So Perkins was put to bed and everybody was awfully nice to him. Dr. Jones fixed up a board so Perkins could play with his Erector Set in bed. Mrs. Jones read Perkins his favorite story six times straight through without even skipping any of the words. And they all spoke to him with that kind of cooing voice which people who are up and about reserve for people who are down in one place.

Allie came up a little later.

"How 'bout some nice hot chocolate," she said. "Somebody stole the brains."

"What was that?" asked Dr. Jones.

"I said," began Allie patiently, "how 'bout some nice. . . ."

"Never mind about the hot chocolate for now, Allie," said Dr. Jones. "What was the second thing."

"I said," began Allie all over again, "somebody stole the brains we was going to have for dinner. Mrs. Jones said make a nice wine sauce. . . ."

"Thank you, Allie," said Dr. Jones.

"Perkins," said Mrs. Jones, gulping. "Did you eat . . . all of it . . . uncooked?"

Her son nodded miserably.

"Well, now," smiled Dr. Jones, "do you feel any brainier?"

Perkins considered his failure momentarily. Then suddenly he brightened.

"Maybe I didn't get any brainier in the head," he said cheerfully. "But I sure gave my stomach a lot to think about."

3. PERKINS THE BRAIN

One of the things that Perkins had that he liked best was a pair of spurs. He had sent two box tops, a quarter, and dime to a cereal company, and they had sent back the spurs. They had also sent a very nice letter telling how you could get a horse.

"Spurs are for riding horses with, aren't they, Daddy?" Perkins had asked.

"Generally speaking," his father had replied.

Perkins showed the letter to his father and watched his face carefully while he read it. Dr. Jones's expression was not exactly what you could call enthusiastic.

Perkins tried looking hopeful. He tried looking sad. He tried looking crushed.

"No," said Dr. Jones. He looked quite cheerful.

"There are," said Dr. Jones, "other uses for spurs."

"I was sure there would be," said Perkins.

He thought about it awhile, and decided to wear the spurs when he went out the next day. The four kids who were about his own age were yelling in the yard which had the pogo stick. Perkins walked

slowly down the street clanking his new spurs on the pavement. He waited till the yelling stopped before clanking around the corner of the hedge into full view.

For a moment everybody looked at everybody else. Then everybody just sort of looked at nothing in particular.

Then Henry said, "What are you wearing those

spurs for?" He was the Henry who had run so fast the day before.

Then Perkins said, "They make other people talk to me first."

"Don't believe you," snickered Henry.

So Perkins said, "Who spoke to who first about why they were wearing spurs?"

"Oh, that," sniffed Henry.

But everybody else could see that the spurs had worked, and they looked at Perkins with a certain amount of interest.

"I'm Bertie," said the smallest boy.

"Bertie?" said Perkins out of the side of his mouth. "Bertie the What?"

"What do you mean, Bertie the What?" said Henry. "His name's Bertie like my name's Henry. There aren't any What's."

"Oh," said Perkins. "That's too bad."

"What's so bad?" asked Bertie, interested.

"Well, there's more to you than just Bertie," answered Perkins.

"Yeah?" said Bertie, looking around him to see if there was maybe something he had missed.

Perkins was beginning to relax. He felt he certainly had made an impression, since they were all asking him questions and he knew you didn't ask a person a lot of questions unless that person had made a pretty good impression.

"Now take Henry," said Perkins, in the casual tone of voice he had when he knew everybody was listening to him anyway.

"I'm Charles," said the boy whose front yard they were in.

"You can borrow his pogo stick if you want to," said Elmer, who was the other boy.

"His name is Elmer," said Charles.

"Hello," said Perkins. "Elmer the What?"

"You were saying, take Henry," said Henry.

"Well," said Perkins, "yesterday I was watching you."

Henry felt important. He had never been *watched* before.

"I was watching you run," continued Perkins. "You run fast. Extremely fast. You might be the fastest runner I have ever watched."

Henry puffed up a little and did a couple of quick turns about the yard.

"Of course, I'd have to watch you again to make sure," said Perkins, "but you are probably Henry the Fast."

"Let's watch him now," said Elmer and Charles together.

They all lined up against the hedge. Henry ran down the street. He ran up the street. Everybody watched him. Henry was getting pink in the face, but he ran down the street a second time. Everybody was still watching him, so he ran all the way back again. He stopped in front of the hedge and looked at Perkins out of the corner of his eye.

Perkins nodded. "You are Henry the Fast," said Perkins solemnly.

Suddenly Elmer began to jump. He just jumped

up in the air two or three times at first. Then he jumped down four steps from the front porch. He jumped over a rose bush. It was a low rose bush, but it had thorns and everything, so it was a pretty daring jump. He jumped over Bertie who was sitting in the grass. Then he did a lot of backwards jumps back to where everybody was standing near the hedge.

"Okay," said Perkins. "Elmer is Elmer the Jump."

Perkins looked around. "We could certainly use a climber around here. Climbing things can be pretty useful."

"Yes," agreed Henry. "That's certainly right." Naturally, he didn't have to do any climbing since he was Henry the Fast and had a lot of running to do.

"Sure could use a climber," echoed Elmer, giving a few extra jumps to make sure everybody remembered just who he was.

"Bertie's kind of small to do much climbing," said Perkins.

So that left Charles, and they all looked at Charles. Then they looked at the tree in Charles's front yard. Then they looked back at Charles again. It took a lot of looking back and forth from the tree to Charles and from Charles to the tree, before Charles understood what all that looking meant.

"Okay," said Charles.

He climbed up to the first branch and then up

a couple more branches for good measure. Then
he got a good grip and peered down through the
branches to make sure everybody was watching.
Everybody was. So Charles hung from the branch
with one hand, which was the bravest thing anybody had done yet.

"Yea, Charles," shouted Perkins.

So they all yelled, yea Charles, and then Charles
came down.

"Am I Charles the Climb?" asked Charles.

"Yep," said Perkins.

"Now it's Bertie's turn," said Henry.

Bertie shook his head.

"Don't you want a name?" scoffed Henry.

"Got a name," said Bertie. "I'm Bertie the What." Bertie pointed at Perkins. "He said so."

"What does What mean?" said Elmer. "*What* doesn't mean anything."

"Hey," said Charles all of a sudden. "What's your name?" He was looking at Perkins.

"I'm Perkins," said Perkins.

"Perkins the What?" asked Charles.

"No, I'm the What," said Bertie.

Everybody ignored him.

"Yeah," said Henry. "You haven't done anything."

"I haven't done anything!" said Perkins slowly. "I thought of the whole idea."

"That's true," said Henry.

"Well, what do you call someone who thinks up ideas?"

"Brainy," said Henry.

Perkins smiled. He felt pretty good. "That's just exactly who I am."

"Who?" said Henry.

"Perkins the Brain," said Perkins.

4. PERKINS HAS AN IDEA

For the rest of that afternoon, the gang had a very good time. Henry ran around a lot. Elmer practiced jumping off the porch steps, then off the porch, and he was beginning to eye the second-floor window. Charles spent most of his time in the tree. And Bertie was saying "What" every time you spoke to him and sometimes even when you didn't. Perkins felt just fine being a member of the gang. He felt fine about being the brainiest, too, because when he said something, everybody else listened.

"Hey," said Perkins.

"What?" said Bertie.

"I gotta go home for dinner," said Perkins.

Henry, Charles, and Elmer listened very carefully.

"See you later," said Henry solemnly.

The next morning, Perkins was sitting in his new room, tying all his string together, when his mother called up from downstairs.

"There's someone here to see you, Perkins dear. With a shovel."

"Oh, that's my best friend Henry the Fast," said Perkins. "With his shovel."

"Yes, I'm his best friend Henry the Fast," said Henry. "With my shovel."

"Er . . . naturally," said Mrs. Jones weakly. "Well, do go on upstairs, Henry."

"Henry the Fast," corrected Henry.

"Take your shovel," said Mrs. Jones.

Perkins was on the floor with a pile of string and a pencil on one side of him and two large maps on the other. One was a map of Texas and the other of Bertie's back yard.

"They don't look much alike to me," said Henry.

"Sure they do," said Perkins. "Texas is a big place, isn't it?"

"Yeah," said Henry.

"Which means it's got a lot of dirt in it, doesn't it?"

"Yeah," said Henry.

"Bertie's yard is pretty big, too, isn't it?" said Perkins.

"Yeah," said Henry. "Can I put my shovel down?"

"Sure," said Perkins. "Which means there's a lot of dirt *there,* too."

Henry put his shovel on the floor and looked interested.

"So if you want to find oil, all you need is a lot of dirt to dig in," finished Perkins.

Henry sat himself on the floor and looked convinced.

They studied the map of Texas. Then they studied the map of Bertie's back yard. Bertie's parents were going to be away for the day. Henry's mother was going to keep an eye on Bertie. But since Bertie lived three houses away from Henry's house, Henry's mother couldn't possibly keep an eye on Bertie's *house* all day. Anyway, that was how Perkins figured it. He thought it was too great an opportunity to miss. Probably the last chance any of the gang would have for a long time to get rich.

"Bertie's mother is sure going to be mad," said Henry.

"She won't be mad," said Perkins confidently. "We'll give her some of the profits and she can buy a hundred new back yards."

"That's true," admitted Henry.

Perkins stuffed the string and the pencil into his pocket and rolled up the maps. Then they went over to get Elmer and Charles, who were at Charles's house taking turns on the pogo stick. Then they went over to Elmer's house to get another shovel and a package of caramels that Elmer had. Then they all went down the street to Bertie's house.

"Boy, my mother is sure gonna be mad," said Bertie, when Perkins had explained what they were going to do. "I better not let you do it."

"Here's a package of caramels, Bertie," said Perkins.

Bertie accepted the bribe immediately. "Well, you can do it," said Bertie, "but my mother's still gonna be mad." Then he didn't say anything else because his jaws were stuck together with caramel.

"Where is the oil in Texas?" asked Henry, looking at the map.

"In the south part," said Perkins.

"Where do you think is the best place to start digging in Bertie's yard?" asked Elmer.

"Behind that tree," said Perkins, pointing to the far end of the yard.

"Because it's south?" said Elmer.

"No," answered Perkins. "Because nobody can see us."

When they were all behind the tree, Perkins handed Henry Henry's shovel, and he handed Charles Elmer's shovel.

"Henry'll want to use his own shovel, naturally," said Perkins.

"Naturally," said Henry.

"But I thought," continued Perkins, "that maybe Elmer would lend Charles the other shovel for a while and take turns."

"Okay," said Elmer. "But gee, Perkins, you won't have a shovel then."

"Oh, that's okay," said Perkins. "I'll just fool around with the pogo stick for a while. I don't mind."

It took everybody else a couple of hours' worth of digging and scraping their hands and getting sore in their arms to discover that even if Perkins didn't mind not digging, they minded him not digging.

"Hey," said Henry, "why 'on'tchu c'movandig a lilbi'."

"What'd you say?" said Perkins.

Henry took some of the dirt out of his mouth so he could talk a little better. But just then, Perkins started to wave his arms with a great deal of enthusiasm. He said a lot of things like:

"Hey, that's the biggest hole I ever saw," and "Gee, that's a great hole," and "I don't think I ever saw a better hole in my whole life," and "Boy, this is the best digging gang in the world."

Just then their mothers called them in for lunch, which saved anybody's digging for a while.

Perkins put on his Roy Rogers hat before he came down to the table He had gotten it at a rodeo when he was six. It was a little small, but he liked the way it rode nice and easy on top of his head. And when Perkins got downstairs, and his mother said to his father,

"Dear, don't you think we might get Perkins another hat? That one's getting awfully small," Perkins replied,

"Oh, that's all right. Can't be helped if my brains are getting bigger all the time."

When the gang got back to the hole, Perkins tied a rock on the end of his string and dropped it down. After the rock hit the bottom, Perkins marked the string with his pencil to show how deep the hole was. Then he pulled the rock out, placed it at Bertie's feet, and pulled the string tight.

As it turned out, the hole was bigger than Bertie and Charles, but not so big as Henry and Elmer.

"Just about my size," said Perkins, which pleased him for no reason at all. "We better dig some more."

So they dug some more.

Then suddenly Henry said, "Hey, we hit something. There's something here."

Perkins squeezed down into the hole. "Sure did," yelled Perkins. "H'ray for Henry."

Perkins grabbed the shovel and started whacking at whatever the thing was. Then Henry whacked. Then Elmer and Charles whacked. Even Bertie whacked at it. They really enjoyed all that whacking.

Soon they began to notice that the dirt down there was getting awfully squashy. The hole was even beginning to cave in a little at the bottom. It smelled different, too.

"Well, Bertie," said Perkins, in that casual way he had, "we better go see if your father is home yet."

"What do you mean?" said Henry.

"Oil," said Perkins. "And we'll need a pump. And derricks. And trucks. And shovels. And tanks." Then he added, "And new hats." Perkins was already seeing his picture in all the newspapers. "It can get very noisy, all that stuff going on," said Perkins, "so I think we better explain about it to Bertie's father."

Suddenly Charles understood what was happening, and yelled "OIL!" at the top of his voice. Soon they were all yelling it.

Bertie was still sitting at the bottom of the hole. "My mother's sure gonna be mad," he was saying.

When Bertie's father came home, he looked first at the hole, then at the gang. Then he stared down

again into the hole. The first thing he saw in the
hole was his son, who was dirty and wet and beginning to feel rather lonely down there by himself.
The next thing Bertie's father saw was that his fuel
pipe had been broken, and the oil he used to heat his
house, so that Bertie and his mother stayed warm,
was spilled all over the ground.

Perkins watched Bertie's father staring down the
hole. So Perkins went over and stared down the
hole, too.

"Oil," said Perkins. "We discovered oil." He
wasn't quite sure why, but somehow this time he
didn't exactly feel like yelling about it.

Later, when Perkins was being spanked for digging a great big hole in Bertie's mother's back yard
and for breaking Bertie's father's fuel pipe, he still
didn't feel too bad about the whole thing. After all,
he had discovered oil, hadn't he? And if they'd let
him, he might have made everybody in the town
very rich. Even after the spanking was over, he still
felt good about it. But when Perkins finally understood that Bertie's father had actually *paid* for the
oil to be put there in the first place, he was terribly
upset.

"You mean it wasn't brand new oil growing in the
ground, Daddy?" asked Perkins.

"It was not," said his father. "Bertie's father put
it there on purpose."

Perkins sat up in bed which was where he had been put after the spanking.

"You mean if Bertie's father hadn't put the oil there, I'd really have discovered oil?" he asked.

"That's right," said Dr. Jones.

Perkins squirmed down under his blankets feeling much better. If Bertie's father hadn't gone and put all that oil in his back yard he, Perkins, would be a famous discoverer by now. It had been Bertie's father's fault after all.

5. PERKINS
HAS ANOTHER IDEA

Perkins had a lot of other good ideas, too, besides digging for oil. There was the day, for instance, when he was watching the older kids squirt each other with the garden hose. They were having a fine time, and Perkins wouldn't have minded a squirt or two himself. Perkins didn't know three of the older kids, but the other one was George. One day George had said to him,

"Hello, kid, how're you doing?"

And Perkins had said, "Fine, how are you doing?" So Perkins felt he knew George pretty well.

It was George's turn to be squirted, when his mother called,

"George, I'm going shopping. You'll have to watch your sister for me."

George's sister was Baby Susan. Baby Susan was a year old. She wasn't much to talk to, but she could blow the best spit bubbles on the block.

"Gee whiz," said George. "I'm beginning to feel like a sandwich. I've got a big sister on top and a

baby sister on the bottom and I'm the cheese in between."

Perkins thought it must be terrible to feel like a sandwich. So he said to George,

"You go get squirted. I'll watch Baby Susan."

"Hey, that's swell of you, Perkins," said George. "I won't forget it."

George was right. He wouldn't forget it.

Because when Perkins went across the street where Baby Susan's playpen was out in the front yard, he got to thinking. It was really too bad about George feeling like a sandwich. In the other houses that had kids, they had two kids. Except for George's house which had three. And his own house.

"There's just me at our house," said Perkins.

Which was what gave Perkins the best idea he had ever had. Of course, he'd have preferred Baby Susan to be Baby John or Baby William or even Baby Perkins, but a girl was better than nothing at all. What he figured was that there had been some mistake. His mother and father hadn't moved to the new place in time, so they had given the extra baby to George's house instead. Well, Perkins would fix everything up. He could take Baby Susan home now and explain about the mistake to George's mother later on. And George wouldn't have to feel like a sandwich any more.

"How would you like to come home with me, Baby Susan?" asked Perkins.

"'Es," said Baby Susan.

Baby Susan said yes to everything because it was the only word she could say. But Perkins didn't know that, so he picked her up out of the playpen and carried her home. He could hear his mother and Allie out in the kitchen, but he thought he would wait until his father got home and surprise everybody at once. So he lugged Baby Susan up to his room and put her on the floor.

Perkins sat and watched her awhile, but she didn't do anything very interesting. He tried getting her to help him build a garage with his Erector Set, but all Baby Susan did was suck on the pieces. So Perkins built the garage himself and let Baby Susan watch.

Then he tried showing her the pictures he had cut out of magazines and pasted in his scrapbook. Baby Susan didn't seem too interested in that either.

But when Perkins handed her the jar of paste, Baby Susan cooed and blew the biggest bubble she had ever blown. She put her fat little fist into the jar. Then she looked at it awhile. Then she put it in her mouth.

"'Es," said Baby Susan.

Perkins looked doubtful. "Are you sure your mother lets you eat paste?" asked Perkins.

"'Es," said Baby Susan.

"Well, okay, then," said Perkins. "But it'll probably make your liver stick to your kidneys."

"'Es," said Baby Susan.

"And your kidneys stick to your ribs," said Perkins.

"'Es," said Baby Susan.

"And your stomach stick to your heart," said Perkins.

"'Es," said Baby Susan.

"Okay, if you want to be all stuck together," said Perkins, "it's all right with me."

It was when there wasn't any more paste that Perkins's troubles began. Baby Susan's face crinkled up. Baby Susan's mouth opened very wide. And then Baby Susan let out the loudest noise Perkin's had ever heard.

"C'mon, Baby Susan," begged Perkins. "Not so loud. You want everybody to hear you? You're supposed to be a surprise."

To stop Baby Susan from crying, Perkins tried

everything. He made funny faces. He turned a couple of somersaults. He brought her a glass of water. He even found another jar of paste.

But Baby Susan was tired of paste, and besides she wanted to go home. So she kept right on crying.

Naturally it wasn't very long before the door to Perkins's room opened and his mother and father walked in.

"Surprise," said Perkins. "Isn't this a nice surprise?"

For some reason, his parents didn't look quite as pleased as Perkins thought they would. He thought maybe it was because Baby Susan didn't look so pretty when she was crying, and he wished she would stop.

"She looks much better when she isn't crying," explained Perkins. "She's really very nice when she isn't crying."

He patted Baby Susan's hair so it would look neater and wiped her face with his hand. But Perkins's hands were never exactly clean, so now, on top of the paste which Baby Susan had smeared all over her mouth and the tears which were running down her cheeks, she had black smudges besides. Perkins was feeling discouraged, but he thought he'd try again.

"She won't cost very much to keep," said Perkins hopefully. "All she eats is paste."

Mrs. Jones had been too shocked to say anything at first, but now she wailed,

"Oh, Willoughby!"

Perkins knew his mother only called his father Willoughby when she was terribly upset, and he wondered if it had something to do with the paste.

"If paste is too expensive," said Perkins, "I bet she could learn to eat something else. Couldn't you, Baby Susan?"

Baby Susan only yelled louder.

Afterwards, when Baby Susan had been returned to George's mother, and Perkins had been made to apologize, Dr. Jones called Perkins into the living room. He had only one word to say. The word was,

"Why?"

"You mean why did I bring Baby Susan here?" asked Perkins.

"That's just exactly what I mean," said Dr. Jones.

"To surprise you," said Perkins.

"We were surprised," said his father, dryly. "Why else?"

"Because George had one sister on top and another on the bottom and he said it felt like a sandwich and he was the cheese," said Perkins.

"So you thought if you took the bottom part away, George could stop being the cheese," said Dr. Jones.

Perkins nodded.

"You sound as crazy as your son, Willoughby," said Mrs. Jones, "with all this cheese business. Please just explain that he mustn't ever do such a thing again."

"I think Perkins understands that," said Dr. Jones. "Don't you, son?"

"But they made a mistake," said Perkins. "They gave George's house the extra baby because we were too late. Their house has three and our house just has me."

"Well, what would you say if we got you another baby and let George's mother keep Baby Susan?" asked Dr. Jones.

"Oh, darling," said Mrs. Jones, over her knitting needles. "Can we really have another baby?" Darling was what his mother called his father when she was very happy.

Perkins never could really understand why everyone was making such a big fuss over a baby. But when he thought about it later on, he hoped the one his mother and father got didn't eat expensive things like paste, instead of peanut butter like everybody else.

6. THE PROBLEMS OF LIFE

But even if they didn't always work, Perkins went right on having a lot of ideas. He knew his brain must be getting pretty big, with all those ideas in it, and every now and then he would get his mother's measuring tape out of her sewing box and measure his head. Nothing happened for a while, and then one day the measuring tape showed that his head had grown almost an eighth of an inch.

"You just can't hide an important thing like brains," said Perkins.

And that night at the dinner table he said, right in the middle of his mashed potato, "Don't you notice anything different about me? Around the head, I mean."

"Yes, Perkins dear," said Mrs. Jones. "Your hair's gotten thick. You need a haircut."

So Perkins didn't talk much about his head growing after that, but he kept on thinking up new ideas. He thought up a new way for the gang to play Cowboys-and-Indians. Henry was a running Indian. Elmer was a jumping Indian. Charles was a climbing Indian. Bertie was an Indian who said "What" all

the time. Perkins was just the Cowboy—who was
the only one who had a gun, so he just happened to
win all the battles.

Then he thought up a new way to play Hide-and-
Seek. Henry had to run to where he was going to
hide. Elmer had to jump to where he was going to
hide. Charles had to climb to wherever he was going
to hide. And Bertie had to keep on saying "What"
while he was hiding. So, since Perkins was Perkins
the Brain, all he had to do was just *think* of a hiding
place, and whoever was It had to guess where Perkins was thinking of. And naturally, Perkins could
change his mind.

After awhile, there began to be a few troublesome
results of Perkins being Perkins the Brain. It was
Henry's father who noticed it first.

"That child never, but *never*, walks any more,"
said Henry's father to Henry's mother.

Elmer's mother said, "If Elmer doesn't stop jumping while he brushes his teeth, that toothbrush is
going to go right down his throat."

And Charles's father asked Charles's mother a
hundred times why their son felt he had to climb
through the side window to get into the house instead of just walking in the front door like everybody
else.

But it was Bertie's parents who suffered the most.
No matter how hard they tried when they spoke to
Bertie, all Bertie ever said was "What."

"He's forgotten how to talk," groaned Bertie's father. "And it took years to teach him to begin with."

All the parents wrote letters to the teacher at school saying couldn't the school concentrate a little more on things like walking and English and a little less on things like jumping, running, and climbing. The teacher wrote back and said that she wasn't having any trouble about walking and English at school and that there must be something the matter with their home environment. But she also wrote a letter to Perkins's parents saying that for such a bright boy, Perkins wasn't doing too well with his spelling.

What Perkin's father said to Perkins was, couldn't he manage to do something *constructive* now that he had all those brains.

So the next day, when Perkins found an article in a magazine he was reading about Conservation of Wild Life, he asked his father what Conserving meant.

"Conserving means to save," said Dr. Jones.

"Is saving a constructive thing to do?" asked Perkins.

"It certainly is," said his father.

So Perkins went across the street to see whether Henry wanted to be constructive, too.

Perkins and Henry didn't understand too much

about what was in the article because there were so many words in it. What they did understand was that it was very good to save things that were alive.

"'Course, we don't have any bears around here or any good stuff like that," said Henry.

"No," said Perkins, "but we better stick to smaller stuff anyway. Be pretty hard to save a lot of bears at my house."

"Bugs would be easy," said Henry, "and grasshoppers."

"And ants," said Perkins.

"How about roaches and slugs?" said Elmer and Charles, when Perkins had explained about being constructive.

"What?" said Bertie. But he was thinking about saving flies.

Everybody's parents noticed a sudden improvement in the gang. Henry not only stopped running, he practically crawled around. Elmer stood very still while he brushed his teeth, examining all the cracks on the bathroom floor. Charles still climbed, but more often he stayed on the ground—flat on his face on the ground. And Bertie stopped saying "What." In fact, he stopped saying anything, he was so busy looking for flies. Perkins still hadn't passed his spelling, but he was *feeling* more constructive.

And the more ants he collected, the more con-

structive he felt. He figured he was conserving more wild life than anyone had ever conserved before. As a matter of fact, by the end of the week, he had conserved about three jars' full. He felt if he could just

find enough jars, he could conserve the largest number of wild ant life in the whole history of the world.

On Friday morning, Allie announced to Mrs. Jones,

"That Perkins, he's improved himself a whole lot. Don't think you gonna be worrying 'bout him no more." And Allie flicked the duster over the living-room lamp shades with satisfaction.

Mrs. Jones looked up from the desk where she was writing a check for the grocery bill.

"Yep," said Allie. "Every night now, he been coming into the kitchen after dinner and carrying away the milk bottles for me. My old bones ain't what they was, and it's nice to have a young 'un fetch an' carry."

On Saturday, when Dr. Jones came home to lunch, he said, "Dear, I believe we worry too much about Perkins. He's done a lot of growing up this week."

Mrs. Jones looked up from the desk where she was writing a check for the meat bill.

"Yes," said Dr. Jones. "Every day this week he's come by the office and helped to clear away the trash."

"Including the empty bottles?" asked Mrs. Jones.

"Including the empty bottles," said Dr. Jones.

"I see," said Mrs. Jones.

"What do you see, dear?" asked Dr. Jones.

"Wild life," answered Mrs. Jones. "I have a feeling Perkins is conserving wild life."

"Don't be silly, Mary," said Dr. Jones. "There aren't any game preserves around here."

"Oh yes there are," said Mrs. Jones.

Dr. Jones was interested. "Really? Where?" he asked.

"In our back yard and everybody else's," replied Mrs. Jones.

But Dr. Jones only smiled, and his wife let the matter drop.

On Sunday, the matter came up again. Or rather it came down. From Perkins's room.

Perkins's mother and father were finishing their coffee, and Perkins was halfway through his second dessert, when Dr. Jones went suddenly red in the face. Then he went blue. Then he went almost purple. Pretty soon he started to smack his right leg. He smacked his left leg. Then he smacked both his legs at the same time.

Mrs. Jones looked at Dr. Jones as if he were crazy. But after a minute, her face suddenly went red. Then it went blue. Then it went almost purple, and she started to smack her legs, too.

"Oops," said Perkins. Somehow he didn't feel like finishing his second dessert any more.

"What in heaven's name is going on?" shouted Dr. Jones, scratching his left leg.

"Wild life," said Mrs. Jones, scratching her right one.

Dr. Jones looked at the floor. There, advancing toward them, was the longest parade of red ants any of them had ever seen. Dr. and Mrs. Jones followed the trail of ants as they marched through the dining room. They followed the ants as they marched through the living room. They followed the ants as they marched up the front stairs. They followed the ants as they marched through the upstairs hall. Then they followed the ants straight into Perkins's room.

On the floor was a pile of empty bottles. On Per-

kins's dresser were two milk bottles and several
medicine bottles full of red ants. Only somebody
had forgotten to put back the corks.

"Oops," said Perkins, appearing in the doorway.
His father gave him a pretty hard look.

Perkins gave his father a very sweet look. "You
said that conserving was a constructive thing to do,
Daddy."

"I did," said his father.

"What does conserving mean, Daddy?" asked
Perkins.

"Conserving means to sa—. Never mind what
conserving means," shouted Dr. Jones. "What are
you doing with all these ants in your room!"

"Conserving them, Daddy, and you said conserving means—"

Dr. Jones wasn't quite sure at what point it had
happened, but he knew without question that some-
where along the way he had lost the battle.

So what he said was, "Is the rest of the gang conserving red ants, too?"

And he reached for the telephone.

"No," said Perkins.

"Well, that's something, anyway," said Dr. Jones.

"Henry is conserving bugs and grasshoppers,"
said Perkins, counting off on his fingers, "Elmer is
conserving roaches. Charles is conserving . . ."

Dr. Jones began to dial very quickly.

". . . slugs. And Bertie is conserving . . ."

"One more word," said Dr. Jones slowly, "one more word, and I'll conserve you."

But Perkins didn't think he'd like living in a jar, so he didn't say anything else.

7. THE PROBLEMS OF PERKINS

One time, they were all over at Elmer's house. Elmer's father had bought Elmer a Blackbeard the Pirate set, on the condition that he stop stealing the funnies out of the Sunday paper. But that had been last Monday. Now it was Saturday, and the gang was beginning to get a little tired of playing pirates. Particularly since Elmer was always Blackbeard and the only game he could think of was to make everybody else walk the plank. But it was Elmer's pirate set, so there wasn't much the rest of the gang could do about it.

By Saturday, though, Perkins had had just about enough of plank-walking and drowning.

"Elmer," said Perkins, "couldn't somebody else be Blackbeard for a while?" He said it very nicely, but it made Elmer angry.

"I don't need any of your old ideas," yelled Elmer. "Just because you're Perkins the Brain doesn't mean you're the only one with ideas."

Perkins's feelings were hurt, but he tried not to show it. "I didn't mean I wanted to be Blackbeard," he said. "I just said maybe *somebody else* could be Blackbeard. Maybe Henry. Maybe Charles. Maybe even Bertie."

"Hey, that's a great idea," said Charles. "How about Henry being Blackbeard?"

Perkins's feelings were even more hurt. He had hoped somebody would say how about Perkins. But anything was better than walking the plank all the time, so he said, "That would be fine. I bet Henry'll make just about the best Blackbeard there is."

Henry always puffed up whenever people paid any attention to him. He was very puffy now. Almost too puffy to take over the Blackbeard the Pirate set. But he managed somehow.

Only Henry couldn't think of a new way to play pirates either. So the only difference was that now Elmer joined the plank-walkers while Henry wore the eye patch and held the sword. Perkins didn't say a word.

Then after a couple of days of that, Charles got to be Blackbeard the Pirate, which meant that Henry went back to being a plank-walker while Charles wore the eye patch and held the sword. Perkins still didn't say a word.

When it was Bertie's turn, Bertie just wore the eye patch and forgot about the sword, so then nobody even got to walk off the plank. Bertie didn't really understand the game too well.

But Perkins just went right on playing without saying anything at all. His feelings were still hurt, but if they liked their ideas better, that was just fine with him. He'd walk the plank with them until Elmer's Blackbeard the Pirate set wore away to pieces. Too bad the gang couldn't have had some fun with it, but if that was the way they felt, that was the way it was going to be.

Perkins's parent didn't notice it just at first, but Allie noticed right away.

"That child muttering all the day," said Allie.

"Is something the matter, Perkins?" asked Mrs. Jones anxiously.

Perkins shook his head, but he went right on muttering.

"Speak up, son," said Dr. Jones. "Now what did you say?"

"Nothing," said Perkins, and muttered some more.

"Oh well," said Allie. "He just brooding. All children brood time to time."

By the time the next Saturday came around, the gang had had enough. They still wanted to play pirates, but they wanted to play it differently. The only trouble was, none of them could think how. Henry asked Charles if he could think of a new way. Charles said no. Then Charles asked Elmer if he could think of a new way. Elmer said no. Then Elmer asked Henry, and Henry asked Bertie, and

Bertie as usual said "What." None of them mentioned it, but what they really wanted to do was go over to Perkins's house and ask Perkins. They were very sorry about not letting Perkins be Blackbeard the Pirate, and Elmer was sorriest of all. And since everybody in the gang was thinking exactly the same thing, what they did was all run out of Elmer's house together and up the street to Perkins's house.

"Perkins!" they shouted. "Hey, Perkins the Brain!"

Perkins had been sitting in the attic by the window and had seen them leave Elmer's house. He was hoping they would come to his house, even though he wasn't sure they would. And when Perkins heard them shouting his name, he didn't know why, but he started to cry. He felt better than he ever had in his whole life, but he cried anyway.

When he stopped crying, he went downstairs, and Henry put the eye patch on him, and Charles put the sword in Perkins's hand, and Elmer himself said he would be the first one off the plank.

After that, Perkins stopped muttering.

But only for a week.

Because later on, something else happened. It all started when Bertie's mother told Henry's mother, who told Henry:

"Isn't it nice? Another new family is moving into town."

"Any kids?" asked Henry.

"One," said Henry's mother.

That afternoon, Henry told the gang about the new family with one kid that was moving into town.

That evening, Perkins started to mutter again.

He went up to the attic, which was a very good place to be when you wanted to mutter to yourself. Perkins dragged the chair with one leg missing over to the window and looked outside. He wanted to be the first to see the new family when they moved in, and until they came, he was going to sit at that window every chance he got.

One kid, huh, he kept saying over and over to himself. He's probably taller than me, too, so I won't even be the third tallest any more. Or maybe smaller, so I won't be the third smallest either. And if he's older, I won't be the oldest of the younger kids, or the youngest of the older kids. He might be a fast runner, and then Henry won't be Henry the Fast any more, which would be awful because Henry's my best friend.

"Perkins," called Mrs. Jones, "time for dinner."

So Perkins came down for dinner, but after dinner he went right back up to the attic again to look out the window.

He might be the fattest, which wouldn't be too bad, because we don't really have any fat kids around here. Or he might be the skinniest, which wouldn't matter too much because everyone's pretty skinny.

"Perkins," called Mrs. Jones, "bedtime."

So Perkins came down to go to bed, but in the morning he went right back up to the attic again to look out the window.

He might have a bigger bicycle, thought Perkins, even a racer. And anybody who had a racer, figured Perkins, was bound to be mean about lending it. Or he might have sent away for a pair of spurs and then everybody in the gang would have to talk to *him* first.

"Perkins," called Mrs. Jones, "time for school."

Perkins muttered his way to school and then muttered all the way home again. Right back up to the attic.

He was saving the worst thought of all for that afternoon.

The new kid might even—and here it was so terrible that Perkins gulped just thinking about it—he might even have been born with or read about, or sat down and thought about, or eaten so many brains that nobody would ever want Perkins's ideas again.

That night, Perkins even muttered in his sleep.

At breakfast, Mrs. Jones commented to Dr. Jones that the new family seemed very nice, and that Mrs. Phillips and her daughter had just stopped by to say hello.

"Mrs. Phillips and her *what?*" choked Perkins. He was eating his third bowl of cereal. He wanted to finish it up so he could send in the box top for a set of secret voodoo rings.

"Her daughter," said Mrs. Jones. "Janice Phillips

is the prettiest sixteen-year-old girl I've seen in a long time."

Dr. and Mrs. Jones never did understand exactly what happened, but after that morning, Perkins stopped muttering entirely.

8. GIRL TROUBLE

Bertie had a sister named Claire Louise. She was two years older than Bertie which made her the same age as Perkins. But they didn't know each other, because Claire Louise had been away visiting her grandmother ever since Perkins had come.

One morning after breakfast, when Perkins went to look out the kitchen screen door, there were two faces looking back at him. One was Bertie's face, and the other was a girl's face.

"Hello," said Bertie. "This is my sister Claire Louise who is going to our school now instead of the one where my grandmother lives and this is her first day so my mother said couldn't you take her with you since my sister's in the same class you are?"

It was the longest speech Bertie had ever made. When it was over, he ran right home to rest. That left Perkins staring at only one face, but since it belonged to a girl, Perkins didn't know what to do about it. There were only three things he knew about girls. One was that they weren't good for anything at all. The second was that whenever you talked to them they giggled. And the third thing was

that Perkins himself wouldn't be caught dead with one of them.

And here Bertie had gone and just left one on Perkins's back porch. And he was going to have to go someplace with her besides. "I could punch that Bertie right in the nose," grumbled Perkins angrily.

Meanwhile, Claire Louise had gone and sat down on the back steps to wait. "Guess she knows enough to leave a man alone when he has to think," said Perkins to himself. "That's something, anyway."

He picked up his books and went outside. Perkins felt he ought to say something, but all he could think of to say was hello. So he said that.

"Hello," said Claire Louise. She didn't say anything else either, because she suddenly liked Perkins. And if you like a person, you don't have to do a lot of talking. So Claire Louise just smiled.

"At least she doesn't giggle," thought Perkins, "and she hasn't got teeth missing." But he still wasn't about to be seen with any girl.

"Wait here," said Perkins.

Claire Louise waited obediently while Perkins went to look up and down the street. It was early for any of the kids to be going to school yet, so if they left right away nobody would see him.

"C'mon," said Perkins.

"Okay," said Claire Louise.

As they went down the street, Perkins walked very fast, so that Claire Louise was always three or four steps behind him. That way, if somebody saw him, Perkins could pretend he didn't even know Claire Louise was there. Even if she was better than a lot of girls Perkins had seen, he still felt like punching Bertie in the nose.

When they got to school, Perkins brought Claire Louise up to the fourth grade classroom. Nobody was there yet.

"Where shall I sit?" asked Claire Louise.

"I dunno," said Perkins.

Claire Louise got a funny little lost look on her face, which reminded Perkins of how he had felt the first day he had come to school.

So he said, "But you can sit in my seat, if you want to, till you get one of your own."

That made Claire Louise's funny feeling go away. "Thank you, Perkins," she said.

So Perkins felt good, too, until everybody came in and sat down and the teacher was saying,

"It was very nice of you, Perkins, to give Claire Louise your seat."

Then Perkins felt awful, because after that everybody started to giggle and whisper, "Perkins has a girl, Perkins has a girl, Perkins has a girl."

Perkins wanted more than ever to punch Bertie in the nose. At least, thought Perkins, it's over with now.

But it wasn't. After school, there was Claire Louise, waiting for him just outside the schoolyard.

"I want to walk home with you," said Claire
Louise.

Perkins groaned.

"I promise to walk behind you," said Claire
Louise.

"All right," sighed Perkins. "Come on."

When they got to Bertie's house, the gang was
waiting for them.

"Perkins has a girl," they yelled.

But Perkins looked so mad, that pretty soon they
were all yelling something else instead. For a while,
Claire Louise listened, and then she yelled. Everybody turned around. It was the loudest yell they had
ever heard.

"Not bad for a girl, huh?" grinned Bertie. "I told you she was all right for a sister."

After that, the gang did some running. Naturally, Henry was the fastest, but Claire Louise came in second.

Then they had a jumping contest. Elmer jumped the highest, but Claire Louise could jump almost as high. When they took turns climbing up the rain spout, Charles got the farthest up, but Claire Louise got farther than any of the others.

Then when Perkins had a really great idea about a new game to play, Claire Louise said she thought it was the best idea she had ever heard. That, Perkins felt, made Claire Louise the second brainiest, too.

But it was one thing to admit that for a girl, Claire Louise wasn't too bad. It was another thing when Claire Louise appeared at the screen door again the next morning.

"I want to walk to school with you," she said, grinning at Perkins.

"Now wait a minute," said Perkins.

"I promise to walk behind," said Claire Louise.

So Claire Louise walked behind Perkins—all day long. She followed Perkins all over the place. Wherever Perkins went, there was Claire Louise behind him. And the worst of it was, there was nothing Perkins could do. She wouldn't listen when Perkins told her to go away, and you couldn't just punch a girl in the nose in front of everybody.

At recess, Claire Louise got herself on Perkins's softball team. At lunch, she sat next to him and offered him the banana from her lunch box. And all afternoon, she smiled at Perkins across the classroom.

Perkins was dreading the three o'clock bell. It would be the most awful moment of his life. And sure enough, when they were all let out into the yard after school, it started.

"Perkins has a girl, Perkins has a girl, Perkins has a girl."

One of the bigger boys, whose name was Mugs and who was always smarty about everything, said it louder than everybody else and pointed his finger besides.

"Perkins has a girl," he jeered.

Perkins gave Mugs a very long look, starting with Mugs's head and going right down to Mugs's toes and then all the way up again.

"Naturally," said Perkins coolly. "Who doesn't?"

"I don't," said Mugs.

"Oh," said Perkins, in a very sympathetic tone of voice, "that's too bad, Mugs. I'm so sorry."

Then Perkins walked away. Claire Louise followed, walking behind him.

"What're you walking *behind* me for?" said Perkins. "You're my girl, aren't you?"

And right in front of everybody, Perkins marched Claire Louise across the street and home.

After that, nobody said a word. Claire Louise thought she was the luckiest girl in the world. And Perkins thought he wouldn't punch Bertie in the nose after all.

9. OPERATIONS

It was raining out. It was also Saturday. The combination was terrible. It was awful for Allie because the clothes wouldn't dry.

"The whole family is going to have to walk around in just sheets next week, these clothes don't dry," grumbled Allie.

Privately, Perkins thought it would be fun if that happened, but he didn't say so out loud since Allie was upset enough already.

The rain was awful for Mrs. Jones because she had just had her hair done and the dampness was making all her new curls come out.

"I won't have a single curl left," sighed Mrs. Jones, "and we're having company for dinner."

Privately, Perkins thought she looked prettier without curls, and he couldn't see anyway what curls had to do with eating dinner. Still, he didn't say anything about it.

But a rainy Saturday was the worst for Perkins, because he couldn't go outside and he couldn't think of anything to do inside.

He tried pasting pictures from old magazines into

his scrapbook. He tried counting all his marbles and ended up leaving them all over the floor. He tried thinking of something new to build with his Erector Set. Finally, he just gave it up and went downstairs to eat a peanut butter sandwich. Now that he belonged to a gang, it wasn't much fun doing things by himself any more. But here he was, stuck in his house. And there they were, stuck in their houses.

Then Perkins remembered a word they had in spelling the week before. The word was "adjustment." And the sentence they learned it in was, "There ought to be an adjustment in the situation."

There certainly ought, grumbled Perkins to himself, and he went off to find his mother.

"Can I call Henry and see if his mother will let him come over?" asked Perkins.

"I don't see why not, dear," said Mrs. Jones.

Well, thought Perkins, if his mother couldn't see why Henry couldn't come, she probably wouldn't see why Elmer couldn't come. And if she couldn't see why Elmer couldn't come, she probably wouldn't see why Charles couldn't come. Or Bertie. Or Claire Louise.

So Perkins picked up the telephone and called everybody up.

"Can you come over?" Perkins asked Henry.

"I'll find out," said Henry. After a moment he came back to the telephone. "My mother says I have

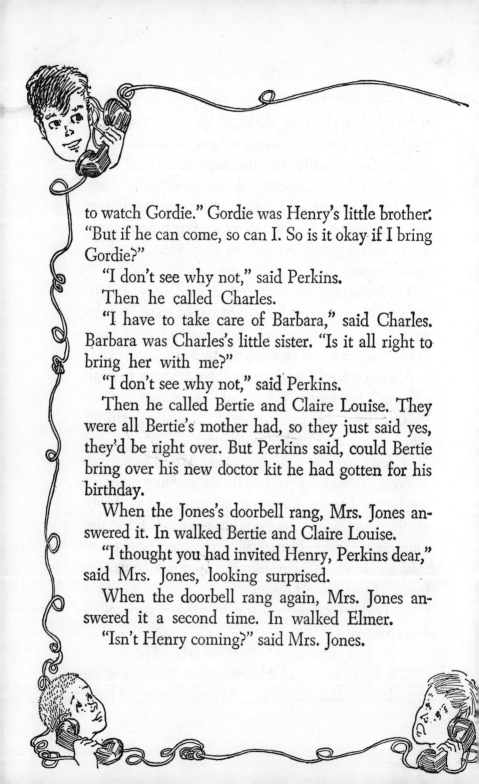

to watch Gordie." Gordie was Henry's little brother. "But if he can come, so can I. So is it okay if I bring Gordie?"

"I don't see why not," said Perkins.

Then he called Charles.

"I have to take care of Barbara," said Charles. Barbara was Charles's little sister. "Is it all right to bring her with me?"

"I don't see why not," said Perkins.

Then he called Bertie and Claire Louise. They were all Bertie's mother had, so they just said yes, they'd be right over. But Perkins said, could Bertie bring over his new doctor kit he had gotten for his birthday.

When the Jones's doorbell rang, Mrs. Jones answered it. In walked Bertie and Claire Louise.

"I thought you had invited Henry, Perkins dear," said Mrs. Jones, looking surprised.

When the doorbell rang again, Mrs. Jones answered it a second time. In walked Elmer.

"Isn't Henry coming?" said Mrs. Jones.

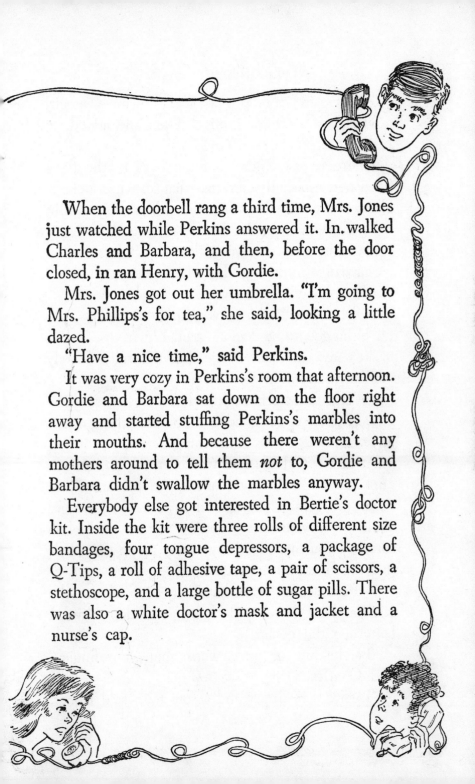

When the doorbell rang a third time, Mrs. Jones just watched while Perkins answered it. In walked Charles and Barbara, and then, before the door closed, in ran Henry, with Gordie.

Mrs. Jones got out her umbrella. "I'm going to Mrs. Phillips's for tea," she said, looking a little dazed.

"Have a nice time," said Perkins.

It was very cozy in Perkins's room that afternoon. Gordie and Barbara sat down on the floor right away and started stuffing Perkins's marbles into their mouths. And because there weren't any mothers around to tell them *not* to, Gordie and Barbara didn't swallow the marbles anyway.

Everybody else got interested in Bertie's doctor kit. Inside the kit were three rolls of different size bandages, four tongue depressors, a package of Q-Tips, a roll of adhesive tape, a pair of scissors, a stethoscope, and a large bottle of sugar pills. There was also a white doctor's mask and jacket and a nurse's cap.

"That's in case you happen to have a girl around," said Claire Louise. Then she added, to make sure, "Like me."

Claire Louise knew that the boys in the gang liked her, especially Perkins—that is, when nobody else was around. But when they all got together in a bunch, Claire Louise had to remind them every single time that she was still alive. Sometimes, it got awfully annoying, but there wasn't anybody else to play with.

"Okay," said Perkins, "you can be nurse."

"Who gets to be doctor?" said Elmer.

"It's my kit," said Bertie, but naturally nobody paid any attention to that.

"Well," said Perkins, "the doctor is the healthiest one. He doesn't get bandaged up or anything or get any of the sugar pills or anything."

At first everybody had wanted to be doctor, but after what Perkins said about the bandages and sugar pills, they changed their minds. Bandages could be very useful in getting mothers to feel so sorry for you that they let you stay up an extra half hour, with seconds in dessert besides.

"Of course, my finger has really been hurting the last couple of days," said Henry, "so I don't think I better be the doctor."

"Betcha my toe hurts worse than your finger," said Charles.

"I got a sore finger and a sore toe," said Elmer.

As long as he was going to be bandaged, he might as well have it done in as many places as possible.

"Guess I'll have to be doctor, then," said Perkins, which is what he had hoped would happen all along. He figured he could always eat a sugar pill or two afterwards, if he felt like it.

"Isn't anybody going to ask me?" said Bertie.

"Sure," said Perkins. "What's bothering you, Bertie?"

"It's my kit," said Bertie.

"What Bertie means is his stomach," explained Claire Louise.

Bertie shook his head. What Bertie meant was it was his kit and nobody had even asked him if he wanted to be doctor. As far as he could see, that had nothing to do with his stomach. So he made a face.

"See," said Claire Louise. "It's his stomach. Even his face looks like his stomach hurts. Better take some sugar pills, Bertie."

"Hey," said Perkins. "Who's the doctor around here, anyway?"

"You are," said Claire Louise.

"Okay then," said Perkins. "You get the water, Claire Louise, and I'll give out the pills."

"How about my finger?" said Henry.

"And my toe?" said Charles.

"And my finger *and* my toe?" said Elmer.

So first Henry and Charles and Elmer got about three yards of bandage wrapped around their fingers

and toes and had lots of adhesive tape stuck on to make sure the bandages would last.

Then it was Bertie's turn. First he got his temperature taken. Then he had to stick his tongue out and say a-a-a-ah. Then he got his back thumped while Perkins listened to Bertie's heart with the stethoscope. And then he got his stomach poked to see where it hurt.

Bertie wasn't exactly comfortable during all of this, but for a change, at least, everybody was paying some attention to him, which made him happy.

"As your doctor, Bertie my boy," said Perkins, "I recommend two pills every five minutes—for the

next hour," he added, trying to remember how many pills there were altogether.

"And you have to drink a lot of water with every pill—to make it settle," ordered Claire Louise. She wasn't so sure about the settling part, but since she had filled Perkins's wastebasket full of water, she was absolutely sure she wasn't going to carry it all the way back to the bathroom again.

"Okay," said Bertie agreeably.

Bertie had finished half the bottle of pills and about three-quarters of the wastebasket full of water, when they all had to go home.

Later that evening, the telephone started to ring. The first time it rang, Henry's mother was on the other end of the line.

"Thank you so much, Dr. Jones," said Henry's mother, "for bandaging Henry's finger. I hope it wasn't any trouble."

The second time the telephone rang, it was Charles's mother, who thanked Dr. Jones for bandaging Charles's toes. The third ring was Elmer's mother, telephoning to thank Dr. Jones for bandaging both Elmer's fingers and his toes.

"There must be another Dr. Jones in this house," said Dr. Jones, looking straight at Perkins, "who seems to have done an awful lot of bandaging this afternoon."

Just then, the telephone rang again.

"Bertie's mother?" said Dr. Jones.

At that point, Perkins felt he might be better off if he moved to another town to practice medicine.

Dr. Jones listened for a while to Bertie's mother talking on the other end of the telephone. Then he said, "Hold the wire just a moment, will you?" and he went over to where Perkins was balancing on the arm of one of the living-room chairs.

"Bertie doesn't seem to be feeling very well," said Dr. Jones. "Do you, by any chance, happen to know what could be the matter with him?"

"Well," said Perkins. "He had a pretty bad stomach ache this afternoon."

"When he came?" asked Dr. Jones. "Or when he left."

"Maybe sometime in between," said Perkins.

"And what did you do for Bertie's stomach ache?"

"Sugar pills."

"And?"

"A little water," said Perkins.

"Oh," said Mrs. Jones, who had been listening to the whole thing. "So that was why your wastebasket was all wet."

"Wastebasket?" said Dr. Jones carefully. "I see."

And he went back to the telephone where Bertie's mother was waiting on the other end.

"I've discovered why Bertie has been going to the bathroom every five minutes," said Dr. Jones, "and I don't think he's got a rare disease at all. What he *has* got is a good dose of sugar pill and water." And when Dr. Jones finished explaining what had happened, he said, "Bertie will be fine tomorrow."

Dr. Jones went back into the living room to talk to the other Dr. Jones who was still balancing thoughtfully on the arm of the chair. Perkins dug into his pocket and fished out what was left of the sugar pills and the roll of bandages.

"I've decided to give up making people well," said Perkins.

"I think that's a very good idea," said his father.

"Now that I've gotten so good at making patients," finished Perkins cheerfully.

10. NO IDEA AT ALL

The day finally came. It was the day Perkins had been dreading for months and months, ever since he had first come to the new place. He knew it had come the minute he woke up that morning. It made

his toes curl. It made his knees wobbly. It made his stomach feel just awful. And Perkins had no idea at all what to do about it. Because that was what the whole problem was. For the first time in all those months, Perkins had woken up without an idea in his head. He couldn't think of anything, not one single thing.

He dressed slowly, because he didn't even have any new ideas about what he wanted to wear. He just put on anything, which happened to be his best navy blue suit and a clean pair of socks, and went downstairs.

"Perkins," said his mother, "Perkins, you darling, you got all dressed up for my birthday today. How very sweet and thoughtful you are." And his mother kissed him on the top of his head.

Perkins gave his mother a small, wobbly smile and went into the kitchen.

"Morning, Perkins," said Allie, "What you want for breakfast?" And Allie waited for Perkins to ask for something nobody had ever eaten for breakfast before, which was what he usually did.

But today, all Perkins said was, "Whatever you think is best, Allie," and sat quietly down at the kitchen table.

Allie simply stared with surprise. "Why Perkins, I declare you're getting to be a big, sensible boy."

After his breakfast, Perkins couldn't think of anything to do, so he just went into the dining room to say good-by to his parents before he left for school. He couldn't even think of something original to say, so he just said Good-by to his father and Good-by and Happy Birthday to his mother.

"He's not himself," said his father, shaking his head. "Not himself at all today."

"He *is* himself," said his mother. "He's a lovely self today." And she smiled, thinking of how nice her son had looked and how polite he was and how he had remembered her birthday.

Sadly, Perkins felt he really agreed with his father. Perkins didn't feel at all like himself. If he had no ideas, he wasn't brainy. If he wasn't brainy, he wasn't Perkins the Brain. If he wasn't Perkins the Brain, he wasn't even really Perkins. And if he wasn't Perkins, he certainly wasn't himself.

When he got to school, it was even worse. He wondered whether he ought to sit in Perkins's seat, since he really wasn't Perkins any more. But nobody seemed to have found out about it yet, so he thought he'd sit there one more day, just for old time's sake, until everybody realized what had happened.

Then at ten-thirty or so, the teacher gave a spelling test. It was terrible. Perkins couldn't think of a new, original way to spell a single word. So he just put down the words the way he remembered them from the spelling book.

That afternoon, the teacher asked him to wait a minute after school. She's going to say who are you,

thought Perkins glumly, but what his teacher said
instead was,

"Perkins, I'm very proud of you. You got every
single word right on the spelling test this morning.
I shall certainly write to your parents about it.
They'll be so pleased."

Perkins walked home, feeling more and more
awful. The gang was all sitting around Charles's
front yard, just the way they were on that first day
a long time ago when Perkins came out to meet
them. But what a difference! The first time he had
so many great ideas to give them. This time he
wasn't even himself, and who wanted to play with
somebody who was nobody.

Perkins had just gotten to the place where you
went around the corner of the hedge into Charles's
yard.

"Hi," said Charles. "What do you think we ought
to do today?"

Perkins was almost sick about what he had to
say, but he was very brave about it. "I . . . don't
. . . know," said Perkins. He was a little pale, but
at least it was over with.

There was a long silence while everybody considered the enormity of the thing.

"*You* have no idea?" gasped Elmer.

Perkins shook his head slowly. "No idea at all."
His voice was sad, but firm. Then he said the next
thing, which was even harder.

"But maybe somebody else has an idea. How about you, Henry?"

Henry was very quiet for a moment. He didn't actually *think* very often, and it was hard work for him.

Finally he said, "Well, do you think maybe we could build a tree house? I bet my mother would let us use the old tree in our back yard for it." When Henry had finished telling his idea, he got red in the face and sat down. It had taken a lot of effort and he wasn't too sure of himself.

But Perkins said right away that he thought it was a wonderful idea, and he even patted Henry on the back. That, of course, made Henry very puffy. But Elmer, who mostly got uncomfortable at new ideas, said,

"Even if we could build a tree house, what would we do with it once we had it?"

Henry didn't have any answer for that. It had been hard enough to think up the tree house in the first place, without having to think what to do with it after it was built.

"I bet you could figure out something pretty good, Elmer," said Perkins.

"I might," said Elmer. It wasn't often he got his opinion asked for, and he wanted to enjoy it. So he thought a minute and carefully broke a stick into two or three pieces and then he said, "We could have meetings in it."

"We sure could," said Perkins enthusiastically.

Then Charles, who was usually shy about saying anything very much, blurted out, "We could keep secret treasures in it."

"That's a great idea, Charles," said Perkins.

Then when Perkins turned around and asked Bertie what *he* thought, the whole gang was surprised. Nobody, but nobody had ever asked Bertie what he thought before. Bertie himself was so delighted he couldn't say anything at all.

"Well," said Perkins. "Maybe Bertie will have an idea after we get started on the tree house."

They were all terribly excited and happy about

the tree house. Everybody was beaming at every-body and slapping everybody on the back.

Until suddenly Elmer said, "There's only one problem."

"What's that?" said Perkins.

"You," said Elmer.

"Oh," said Perkins.

"What do you mean?" asked Henry.

"Well," said Elmer, "Henry is still Henry the Fast because he's the fastest runner. And Charles is still Charles the Climb because he can climb the highest. And I still jump best—"

"What?" said Bertie.

"And you can tell who Bertie is," continued Elmer. "But what about Perkins? He isn't anybody any more because you certainly can't be a Brain if you haven't got any ideas."

"Hey, wait a minute," said Henry, whose head was beginning to work for the first time in his life. "You had a good idea this afternoon, didn't you?"

"Yup," said Elmer.

"And so did I and so did Charles, didn't we? Well, who made us think of those good ideas?"

"Perkins," admitted Elmer.

"Well, what do you call somebody who's so great he can even make other people think up ideas?"

"Brainy," grinned Elmer.

"So who would you say Perkins was?" finished Henry triumphantly.

"Who?" said Charles.

"Himself," said Elmer. "Perkins the Brain."

After that, Perkins gave up worrying about having new, original ideas every minute. Sometimes, it even seemed you did better without them. Providing, he always added, you went about *not* having ideas in a new and original way.